WALT DISNEY PRODUCTIONS
presents

The Aristocats
and the Missing
Necklace

Random House 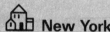 New York

First American Edition. Copyright © 1983 by Walt Disney Productions. All rights
reserved under International and Pan-American Copyright Conventions. Published in
the United States by Random House, Inc., New York, and simultaneously in Canada by
Random House of Canada Limited, Toronto. Originally published in Denmark as
ROQUEFORT HJAELPER ARISTOKILLINGERNE by Gutenberghus Gruppen,
Copenhagen.   ISBN: 0-394-85890-5   Manufactured in the United States of America
34567890   ABCDEFGHIJK

Summer had come, and the city was hot.

It was time for Madame to move to the country.

Away she went in her carriage.

With her went the Aristocats.

There was Duchess, the mother cat.

And there were the three kittens—Tu-tu, Marie, and Berly.

Someone else went along too.

That was Roquefort the mouse.

Everyone was happy to be in
the country.
The kittens explored the yard
and sniffed the fresh country air.

Duchess stayed up in Madame's room.
Madame was dressing for a dinner party.
She sat down at her dressing table
to put on her gold necklace.

Suddenly there was
a CRASH from the room
next door.
"What was that?"
cried Madame.

Madame put down her gold necklace
and went to the door.

The kittens had knocked
a lamp off a table.

"Oh, you naughty kittens!"
said Madame.

Just then a breeze blew
through the rooms.

It sent the curtains flying.

The curtains swept Madame's
necklace off the dressing table
and out the window!

As the necklace
fell from the window,
the goose sisters
walked by.

Swish! The gold necklace landed around the neck of Miss Amelia Goose!

"Why, Amelia, what a lovely necklace!" said her sister Amanda.

"Necklace? What necklace?" said Amelia.

So the geese set off for Mirror Pond so Miss Amelia could see the necklace.

Back in the house Madame
was scolding the kittens.
"No dinner for you tonight!"
she said. "And you'll spend
the night in the kitchen!"

Poor Tu-tu, Marie, and Berly!
They were very unhappy to be shut up
in the kitchen.

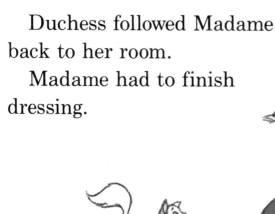

Duchess followed Madame
back to her room.
Madame had to finish
dressing.

Madame went to put on her necklace.
It was gone!
"Have you seen my necklace, Duchess?"
cried Madame.

Duchess
looked under
the dresser.

Madame looked
in every drawer.
No necklace!

Duchess hopped on a table to
look in a deep bowl.

"Get down from there! You'll
break it!" cried Madame. "Oh,
I've had it with cats for today!"

Madame shooed Duchess off to the kitchen.
"You can stay here with your naughty
kittens," said Madame.

"Mama, Mama! What is the matter?"
cried Tu-tu, Marie, and Berly.

"Madame has lost her gold necklace.
She is very upset," said Duchess. "We must
stay in the kitchen until she finds it."

"Oh, what ever can we do?" cried the kittens.

Roquefort the mouse heard the kittens.
He popped out of his mousehole.

"You need a detective," said Roquefort.
"Wait right here!"
And he ran back into his mousehole.

Roquefort put on
his detective hat...

and his detective
coat.

Roquefort Mouse,
the great detective,
was now ready for
action!

"Who will help me
search for the necklace?"
asked Roquefort.
"We will! We will!"
the kittens said.

"Then follow me,"
said Roquefort.
He led the kittens
up the stairs to
the back door.

One, two, three…
the kittens followed
Roquefort through
the small cat door.

Outside Roquefort asked, "Which is the window of Madame's room?"

The kittens showed him.

"The footprints of the thief should be below the window," said Roquefort.

So the kittens helped look for footprints on the ground.

They found lots of footprints.

"Aha!" Roquefort said. "These are goose prints!"

Roquefort and the kittens
followed the goose prints.
The prints went past Frou-Frou,
the carriage horse.

Frou-Frou was laughing and laughing.
"What's so funny?" asked Roquefort.
"The goose sisters just went by,"
said Frou-Frou. "And Amelia Goose was
wearing a gold necklace. Imagine that!"
"Goose! Necklace! Thanks, Frou-Frou,"
said Roquefort. "Come on, kittens. We
have no time to lose!"

They followed the goose prints to
the edge of the woods.

But there the prints disappeared!

"What do we do now?" cried the kittens.

"Let me think," said Roquefort.

Just then two dogs came
out of the woods.
They were laughing and
laughing.

"What's so funny?" asked Roquefort.

"We just met two geese on the path
to the pond," said one of the dogs.

"One goose was wearing a gold necklace,"
said the other dog. "Imagine that!"

"Goose! Necklace! Thanks, fellows!" said
Roquefort. "Quick, kittens. Follow me!"

And off they ran.

The goose sisters had just reached
Mirror Pond.
"Now, Amelia," said Miss Amanda.
"Take a look in the water at yourself."

Amelia leaned over to
look in the water.

Swish! The necklace slid
over her head.

It landed on a lily pad.

"What is that necklace
doing here?" said Amelia.

And the two silly geese
walked away.

Roquefort and the kittens saw
the necklace fall.
"Oh, no!" they cried.
They raced to the edge of the pond.

There was the necklace,
safe on a lily pad.
But it was too far away
to reach.

"Let me think,"
said Roquefort.

Roquefort looked along the water's edge.
He saw a tiny log.
And he saw some dry twigs.
"I think I see a way," he said.

Roquefort broke off
a twig for a pole.
Then he hopped on
the log.

He pushed himself out
to the lily pad...

and pushed the lily pad
back to shore.